Grandpa Stories

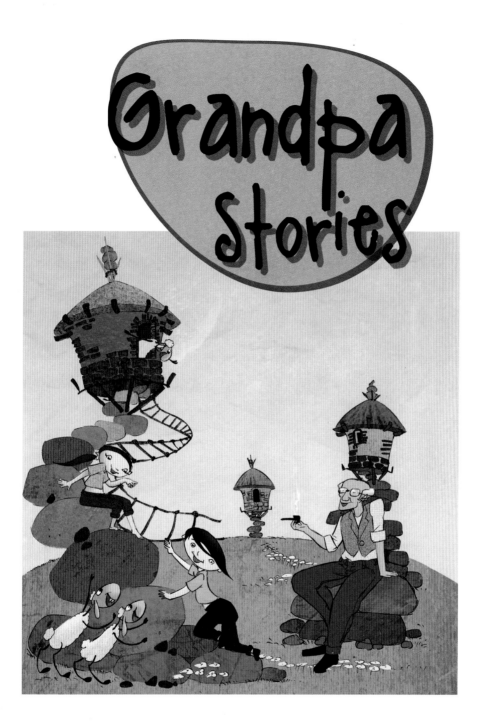

An imprint of Om Books International

Published in 2012 by

OM
KIDZ

An imprint of Om Books International

Corporate & Editorial Office
A 12, Sector 64, Noida 201 301
Uttar Pradesh, India
Phone: +91 120 477 4100
Email: editorial@ombooks.com
Website: www.ombooksinternational.com

Sales Office
4379/4B, Prakash House, Ansari Road
Darya Ganj, New Delhi 110 002, India
Phone: +91 11 2326 3363, 2326 5303
Fax: +91 11 2327 8091
Email: sales@ombooks.com
Website: www.ombooks.com

Content: Subhojit Sanyal
Editor: Sonalini Chaudhry
Illustration: Salil Anand, Kushiram, Jyoti
Design and Layout: Ratnakar Singh

ISBN : 978-93-81607-36-7

Printed in India

10 9 8 7 6 5 4 3 2 1

Contents

Shooting Animals

David had been watching television for quite some time now. His favourite nature show was on. They were showing pictures of wild animals. David loved watching the forest world images. He would always make it a point to be before the television when this programme started.

Grandpa had been sitting with David, watching the show. As the pictures continued, David turned to Grandpa and asked, "Grandpa, who are poachers?"

Grandpa replied, "Why David, they are people who hunt wild animals. It's against the law now, you know!"

David was not pleased at all to hear this. He hated the idea of someone hunting these beautiful animals. "But Grandpa, why would people want to hunt? It is such an evil thing to do!" he exclaimed.

"You *see* that man, David?" Grandpa asked, pointing to the man on the television, who had taken all those pictures of the animals.

"That man's name is Matt. He used to live a few houses away from ours. And you will never believe what he wanted to become when he grew up!" Grandfather explained. "He wanted to be a hunter!"

David was shocked. "But Grandpa," he said, "Matt keeps talking of how evil hunters are. Why would he ever want to be a hunter?"

"Because," said Grandpa, "he never did realise how beautiful animals are. Well, it all happened around his 12th birthday!"

Grandpa then crossed his legs and started telling David the story of Matt, the boy who would always play pranks on animals.

"Matt just loved playing with animals ever since he was young. However, his games were often too rough on the animals. He would tie a string of cans on to his pet dog's tail, or throw stones at the birds on the trees — and once he even dragged his neighbour's cat by the tail.

"His parents were naturally very alarmed to see Matt act this way. They tried explaining to him that animals too should be treated with kindness and respect, but all of that just fell on deaf ears.

"Matt showed no signs of changing his attitude. He would tell his parents that when he grew up, he wanted to shoot animals. His parents were very disheartened on hearing Matt talk like that.

"One day, one of their neighbours, Mr. Waffle came along for a visit. As the elders were talking, Matt ran through the room, chasing his dog. Naturally, Matt's parents were very ashamed.

"Mr. Waffle too was a little shocked to see how Matt was treating his dog. He asked his parents if they knew why Matt was behaving that way with the poor little animal.

"Matt's parents told Mr. Waffle how Matt wanted to grow up and become a hunter. After thinking over the matter for a while, Mr. Waffle called out to Matt and asked him, 'Matt, your 12th birthday is just around the corner. What do you want for a gift?'

"Matt was overjoyed. Without even thinking for a second, he replied, 'Uncle, I would like a slingshot very much!'

'"A slingshot? What on earth will you do with that, my dear boy?' asked Mr. Waffle.

'"Why, I want to shoot animals, Uncle!' said Matt. Mr. Waffle scratched his head for a second and replied, 'So be it, on your 12th birthday, you will surely be able to shoot animals.' Matt's parents looked worried, but Mr. Waffle reassured them that everything would be fine.

"Finally, it was the day of Matt's 12th birthday. Even though most of the guests had already arrived with a lot of gifts, Matt had been particularly waiting for Mr. Waffle to come with his present.

"Soon enough, Mr. Waffle arrived at Matt's birthday party and gave him a wonderfully wrapped box. Matt didn't waste any time in tearing through the ribbons and taking his gift out of the box.

"But lo and behold! Mr. Waffle had not brought Matt a slingshot, but a nice camera. As Matt turned the camera around, Mr. Waffle bent over to him and said, 'Matt, I trust you will be able to shoot some very beautiful animals with this camera. Try it first thing tomorrow morning, ok?'

"Matt agreed to do as Mr. Waffle asked him to. The next morning, Matt clicked some of the finest photographs ever. Most of them were of course, of his pet dog. Ever since that day, Matt enjoyed taking pictures of animals so much that he forgot all about hunting."

And as Grandpa concluded the story, he pointed towards Matt on the television again and said, "And look, today he is one of the finest wild-life photographers of animals."

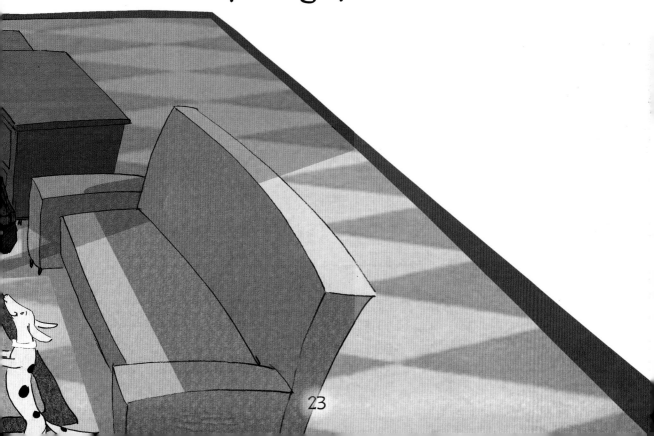

David liked Grandpa's story very much. He declared, "Thank God for Mr. Waffle, Gramps, or Matt would never have shown us such amazing photographs of the wild."

Grandpa hugged David and said, "Had you wanted to be a hunter, my son, I would have to gift you a camera too, you know!"

Three Little Lambs

Robby, David's friend, had paid him a visit. The two of them spent hours talking about how great it would be if they could both go on a camping trip in the woods during their summer vacations.

Just as they were talking of how brave they were and how they were not scared of the wild animals in the woods, Grandpa walked in. The boys told him of their adventure plan.

"Hmm!" said Grandpa, "So you boys want to go out into the woods. What if the big bad wolf catches you at night? What will you do then?"

And then, he began his story...

"Once upon a time, three little lambs lived on a farm. They were bored living the same life everyday. So, they decided to set out in search of some adventure.

They all started walking towards the town on the other side of the woods.

"On the way, the lambs came across a man carrying a huge stack of rainbow-coloured straw on his head. The first lamb walked up to him and asked him whether he could get some straw so that he could build a small little house for himself.

"The man was only too happy to oblige and said, 'Sure little lamb, you can take all the straw you need.'

"The little lamb was very happy with all the straw that he had got from the man. He started building his house at once. Soon, he was living in a very beautiful house made of colourful straw.

"But what the little lamb had not realised was that there was a wicked wolf in the woods, who had spotted the lamb's house and his two brothers.

"The wolf thought to himself, 'My, my, my! This is a fat little lamb. He'd make me a wonderful breakfast. After which I could have his two other brothers for lunch and dinner.'

33

"As he stood outside the magnificent straw house that the lamb had made for himself, he said loudly, 'Little lamb, oh little lamb, please let me in!'

"Naturally, the little lamb was not foolish enough to let an evil wolf into his house. He therefore told the wolf, 'No, no, by the hair of my chinny chin chin, I'll not let you in.'

"But the wolf was not ready to give up so easily and so he said, 'Then I'll huff and puff, till I blow your house in!'

"And so saying, the wolf started to huff and puff and blew as hard as he could, till the house of straw blew away completely.

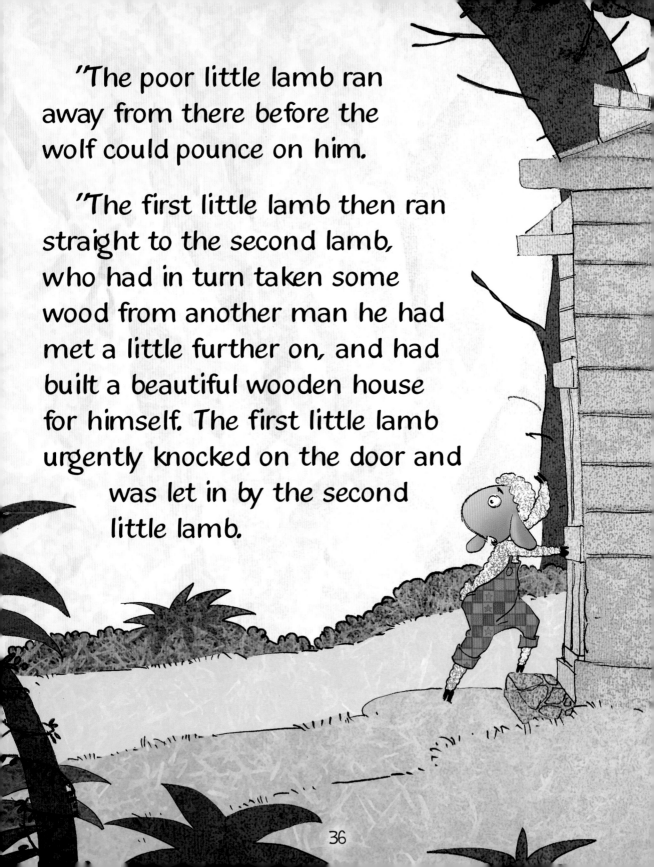

"The poor little lamb ran away from there before the wolf could pounce on him.

"The first little lamb then ran straight to the second lamb, who had in turn taken some wood from another man he had met a little further on, and had built a beautiful wooden house for himself. The first little lamb urgently knocked on the door and was let in by the second little lamb.

"However, the wolf had followed the first little lamb, right to the wooden house of the second little lamb. Seeing that now he could eat the two little lambs together, he said again, 'Little lamb, oh little lamb, please let me in!'

"But the second lamb too knew that he could never let the wolf come inside. He too replied, 'No, no, by the hair of my chinny chin chin, I'll not let you in.'

"The wolf merely replied,
Then I'll huff and puff, till
I blow your house in.'
And so saying, the
wolf huffed and
puffed till the walls
of the wooden
house caved in.

"The poor little lambs ran off towards the third little lamb's house. The third little lamb had very cleverly built a strong house made up of bricks. He let his two brothers come in at once.

"But the wolf arrived there too. He asked the third little lamb to let him in, and when the third little lamb refused like his first two brothers, the wolf started to huff and puff once again.

"But however, much he tried, the wolf could just not blow down the third little lamb's brick house.

"The wolf realized that the brick house would not come down. So he decided to trick the third little lamb to come out instead, where he could easily pounce on him. So the wolf peeped through the window and said, 'Oh little lamb, the farmer next door has some very tasty turnips on his farm. Should we go and get them tomorrow in the morning?'

"The third little lamb loved to eat turnips. But he also knew that the moment

he would step out of the house, the wolf would eat him up. Therefore, the lamb left for the farm before the wolf was supposed to come and came back well in time with all the turnips.

"The wolf was naturally very angry about being made a fool of. He realized that the third little lamb was indeed very intelligent and that he would not fall for the wolf's traps. Therefore, the wolf climbed the third little lamb's house and threatened to come down through the chimney.

"But the third little lamb was smarter than that. He, assisted by his two brothers, kept a cauldron of hot water in the fireplace, and as the wolf jumped down, he fell straight into the pot of boiling water!

"The three little lambs then put a lid on the cauldron, so that the wolf could not come out and then lifted the vessel and threw it down the side of the hill. The wicked wolf was never heard of again."

David and his friend were both rolling on the floor with laughter as Grandpa finished telling them the story. Between laughs, David told Grandpa, "Don't worry Gramps, we shall make a tent of bricks, so that the wolf cannot huff and puff it away!"

The Christmas Present

Christmas time was a busy time for David and his family. There were gifts to be bought, the tree needed to be decorated. All the arrangements needed to be done well before Christmas Eve. But even with the hectic rush, Christmas was always a time of great joy and merriment.

However, when David came back home a few days before Christmas, with a big sulk on his face, Grandpa knew that something must have been wrong. He, therefore, went to David and asked him if something was the matter.

David looked very gloomy and in a very low voice replied, "Grandpa, there were some poor boys outside the bakery, looking at all the delicious pastries. I don't think they had enough money to buy anything. Its just not fair that we can buy anything we want, but some people can't even get a simple plum cake for Christmas."

Grandpa was very touched on hearing David's concerns. He knew that the only way David's mood could be made better was by telling him a story. So he sat down on his armchair and began telling David a tale about Christmas.

"There once lived a little girl called Pam, quite like you, David.

53

"She had been doing her Christmas shopping, when she saw two poor boys walking away from the toy store, with absolutely nothing in their hands.

"Feeling sorry for them, Pam followed the two boys to their home.

"She peeped through a window and saw how the boys were playing happily with each other, as their mother tried to clean up the house before Christmas.

"Pam decided that she would buy the kids some toys, and also something for their mother, so that she too could have a very merry Christmas.

"So the very next day, Pam ran down to the stores and bought all that she could. She got the stores to deliver all the goods to the boys' home on Christmas Eve. Everything went according to plan.

"Finally, it was Christmas day. Even as Pam opened all the gifts that Santa had brought for her the night before, she wanted to know how the two poor boys and their mother were reacting to all the gifts that she had sent for them.

"She went to their house, and, as Pam tried to peep through the ajar window, she saw that the boys were still playing with themselves, and their mother was too was a part of their games.

And not just that, Pam saw that the three of them were playing with the boxes in which all her presents had come!"

Grandpa then bent forward and told David, "Happiness comes from love and

sharing, David. And that is the true spirit of Christmas."

The Cotton Seller

One day, David came home and declared that he had decided to go camping all by himself in the woods. Naturally, his parents

did not approve of this one bit and they refused to let him go into the woods to spend a night all by himself.

David was not very happy with his parents' decision. He refused to eat his food or talk to anyone. Right then, Grandpa walked into the room. Seeing David sitting dejected like that, Grandpa asked, "What is the matter, David?"

David told Grandpa the whole story. Grandpa then asked, "But tell me something... Why do you want to make such a dangerous trip all by yourself?"

"Because," replied David, "my friend Johnny

went all by himself. I too want to do the same thing."

The minute he heard this, Grandpa realised that he would have to tell David a story to make him understand how he should not just blindly imitate someone else's actions.

"Alright, David," said Grandpa, "I know what we can do about this. But first, I want you to finish up all that food in your plate, and then I'll tell you a story."

David ate his food and Grandpa began his story...

"Once upon a time, there lived a cotton

farmer called Marcus. Marcus would always work hard in his fields, and he always had the best crop of cotton in all the land.

"But there was one problem with Marcus — he was a big fool. He would believe whatever people would tell him and therefore, people would always cheat him for their own benefit.

"There was one year though, in which Marcus outdid his own foolishness. After a whole year of working in his fields, Marcus left for the city to sell his cotton produce. He packed huge bags full with cotton and carrying them on his back, he started moving towards the city.

"But as he reached the marketplace in the city, people decided to cheat him of such nice cotton. The store-keepers started telling him that his cotton was all dirty and therefore they were agreeing to pay him a very small amount for it.

"Whichever shop Marcus went to, the shop-keepers all complained that the cotton was dirty. Marcus believed them all. He was very disheartened. This year he would not make enough money.

"He went to all kinds of shop-keepers, even vegetable sellers! But everyone was rude to him. Some men were even laughing at poor unhappy Marcus.

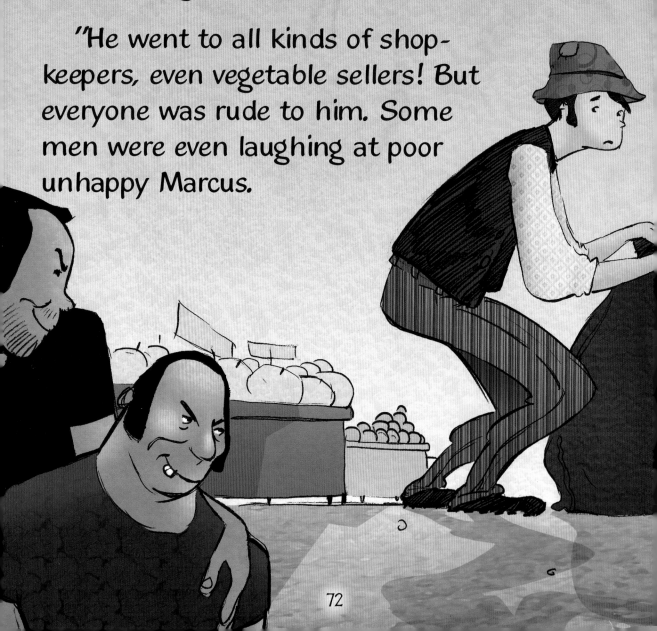

"As Marcus was walking back through the crowded marketplace, he saw a goldsmith burning his gold ornaments.

"Marcus could not understand why the goldsmith would burn his own products.

"So he went up to the goldsmith and asked, 'If you don't mind my asking Sir, why are you burning your gold?'

'Without even bothering to turn his head, the goldsmith replied, 'It is just so obvious... I am burning my gold because I want to purify it and make it cleaner!'

"As soon as the goldsmith informed Marcus about what he was doing, Marcus had a brilliant idea. He decided to burn all his cotton, because like the goldsmith's gold, even his cotton would become clean, white and pure!

"Marcus set all his cotton on the floor, and with a confident stroke, he lit a match and set his entire produce on fire. Needless to say, all his cotton got turned to ashes."

Chuckling, Grandpa then told David, "So you see my son, what is good for one is not necessarily good for someone else. You mustn't blindly follow whatever someone else may have done."

David thought about the story that Grandpa had just told him. Maybe it was not so good an idea to go camping in the woods all by himself after all.

TITLES IN THIS SERIES

   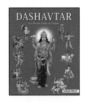 

 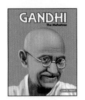   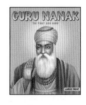